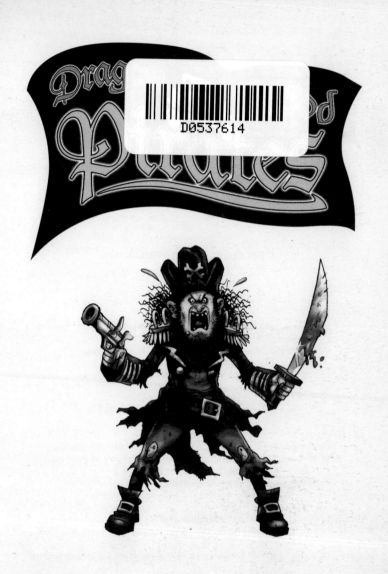

For Brian, bold as a lion

www.dragonbloodpirates.co.uk

ORCHARD BOOKS
338 Euston Road, London NW1 3BH

First published in 2008 by Lothian Children's Books,
an imprint of Hachette Livre Australia
First published in the UK in 2010 by Orchard Books

ISBN 978 1 40831 133 2
(Special price edition ISBN 978 1 40830 738 0)

Text © Dan Jerris 2008
Skull, crossbones and ragged parchment image © Brendon De Suza
Map illustrations on pages 4–5 and on pull-out © Rory Walker, 2008
Pull-out map designed by Kinart
Background map image © iStockphoto.com/Boyce DeGrie
All other illustrations © Orchard Books 2010

A CIP catalogue record for this book is available from the British Library.

10 9 8 7 6 5 4 3 2 1

Printed in Great Britain by J F Print Ltd., Sparkford

Orchard Books is a division of Hachette Children's Books,
an Hachette UK company.

www.hachette.co.uk

Death Diamond

Dan Jerris

ORCHARD BOOKS

Death Island

Shipwreck
Island.

Cannibal
Island

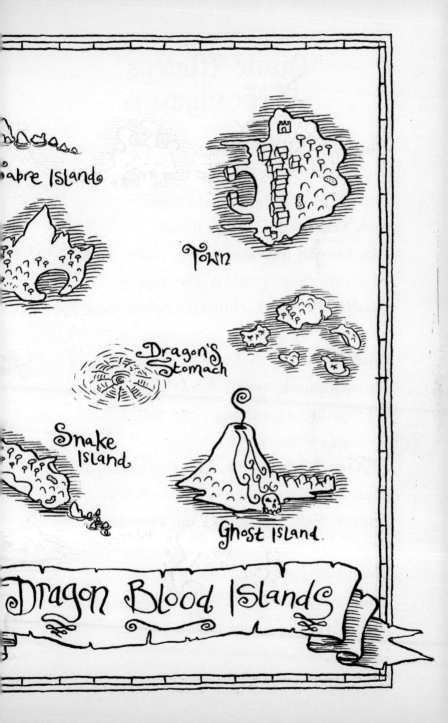

abre Island

Town

Dragon's Stomach

Snake Island

Ghost Island.

Dragon Blood Islands

Pirate Mateys and Scallywags

Alleric (Al) Breas: Lives in Drake Drive and owns a mysterious sea trunk that takes him to the Dragon Blood Islands.

Jack Seabrook: Al's best friend.

Blacktooth McGee: A very nasty pirate who runs the brigantine *The Revenge*.

Flash Johnny: Blacktooth's devious and greedy cabin boy.

Snakeboot: A magical white three-legged cat with purple eyes. Legend has it he once belonged to a terrifying pirate called Vicious Victor.

Pigface McNurt: Blacktooth's bosun; a massive pirate with a ring through his nose.

Snotty Nell: A horrible one-eyed pirate who sails a frigate called *The Tormentor*.

Grenda: Snotty Nell's daughter.

Sharkbait: Snotty Nell's one-legged bosun.

Vampire Zu: Snotty Nell's huge first mate.

Gunner: The pirate captain of the ship *The Booty*.

Mozzy: *The Booty*'s bosun (petty officer).

Slicer: *The Booty*'s cook.

Mahoot: Captain Gunner's cabin boy.

Grandfather: Mahoot's grandfather and guardian of the swimming elephants on Sabre Island.

Stanley Spong: A crooked, sneaky trader who cheats people.

Vicious Victor: A pirate ghost. He used to pillage the Dragon Blood Islands and he stole Prince Alleric's magical sabre.

Prince Alleric: The prince who once ruled Sabre Island but disappeared in mysterious circumstances.

Halimeda (Hally) Breas: Al's younger sister.

Greeny Joe: A shark so big and old that mould grows on his skin, making him glow green in the dark.

Prologue

Al Breas's arms tingled. His feet were wet. Bewildered, he opened his eyes and stared in shock. What was he doing on a rock in the middle of the ocean? Then his friend Jack Seabrook began to appear beside him, shimmering ghost-like for a moment before becoming solid.

Jack's eyes bugged in disbelief as he looked around. "Where *are* we?"

"I have no idea," Al said. He rubbed his

eyes. Only seconds ago he and Jack had been playing in his attic at number five Drake Drive. They'd been drinking cola and Al's dad had been yelling at him to come downstairs and do the dishes.

But Al hated doing chores, and besides, he'd been more interested in the big rusty key he'd just found. When he'd tried it in the lock of the old sea trunk that had once belonged to his grandfather, the mysterious chest had opened.

The sea trunk had been empty, but drawn onto the base was a map of some strange islands. The word **treasure** had leapt out at them, so Al and Jack had leant into the trunk to have a closer look. Suddenly, Al had felt his body go all odd and goosebumpy. He'd clutched the key in his hand and shut his eyes.

Now he was stuck with his best friend in the middle of the ocean on a small rocky outcrop!

"What's *that*?" Jack's eyes bugged out even further. Before them a white ghostly cat appeared. Within seconds the animal solidified just as Jack had done. Wobbling slightly on three legs, its weird purple eyes shone in the sunlight.

Then, apparently terrified, it leapt into Al's lap, mewing pitifully. Al put the rusty key in his pocket and patted the distressed creature.

The tide was coming in and waves swirled around the rock, close to their feet. There also seemed to be a strange green shadow in the water, circling slowly around them. Then a fin cut the surface and Al's eyes widened in fear. "Oh no!" he cried. "A shark!"

The giant creature was so close they could see its cold eyes glowing with menace and green phosphorous mould growing on its ancient skin.

"Help!" Jack and Al both screamed.

The frightened cat clung to Al's tracksuit bottoms and howled, its wail travelling far across the waters.

Just as the waves were lapping at their feet and the shark was sizing them up for dinner, Al and Jack saw a sail in the distance. To their relief, after a few minutes the ship sailed right up to them and dropped anchor.

"It looks like an old Christopher Columbus ship," said Al, waving frantically to the several scruffy men who peered down at them from the ship's rails.

"It's called *The Booty*," Jack spotted, as the ship's patched sails were hauled down and a lifeboat launched.

Seeing the monstrous green shark circling the rock, the men in the lifeboat beat the water with their paddles. The shark thrashed its tail and headed out to sea.

Al and Jack were rescued!

Pirates

"Maggoty biscuits?" said Al in disgust, staring at the plate set before him in the ship's galley.

"Don't you want your dinner?" asked a barefoot boy.

"No, thanks," said Jack.

A tattooed man wielding a knife leered at Jack and Al menacingly. "You'll be sorry," he said.

The barefoot boy grinned, picked up

one of the biscuits and bit into it hungrily.
"Don't take any notice of Slicer," he said.
"My name's Mahoot. I'm the cabin boy, and
let me tell you, there's not much food left.
We haven't found any treasure, you see."

"Treasure?" Al asked, bewildered.

"We've been sailing through the Dragon
Blood Islands for months now," said Mahoot.

"Nothing! But Captain Gunner did say our luck would change." He pointed to the three-legged cat, which now sat curled up in a corner of *The Booty*'s galley. "When we heard a strange howling, Captain Gunner followed the sound and we found you. I reckon if you hadn't had that furball with you, the captain would have left you there to be eaten by old Greeny Joe. This ship doesn't need two more mouths to feed, that's for sure."

"What's so important about the cat?" Al asked.

"Snakeboot's a sea-going cat," Slicer replied. He reached out and tickled the cat under the chin.

"Snakeboot?" said Jack.

"There's this legend," explained Mahoot. "A cat exactly like yours belonged to a famous pirate called Vicious Victor, who died ages ago. A snake bit the cat and the cat chewed its own leg off rather than die from the poison. So Vicious Victor called it Snakeboot."

"A pirate's cat?" said Jack.

"With a cat like that," said Slicer, "we'll get lucky and rich. *And* he'll keep the rats down."

No sooner had Slicer spoken than a strong wind howled through the rigging and *The Booty* rolled to one side. The plates on the table clattered to the floor.

"Storm approaching!" screamed the bosun from above.

"We'd better find you a place to bunk down," said Mahoot. "The storms around here can be fierce. And you boys don't look like you have your sea legs yet."

The storm raged and the ship rolled and pitched. The boys sheltered in the dank hold, which stank of sewage and rats. Between stomach-heaving swells and violent seasickness, Jack peered at Al with red-rimmed eyes and said, "I want to go home."

Al agreed, but there was nothing they could do. They were stuck on a ship with what appeared to be pirates, in a place called the Dragon Blood Islands...

Death Island

When the tossing seas quietened, Al and
Jack made their way unsteadily to the deck.
Al squinted in the sunlight and looked
around. *The Booty* was anchored in a cove,
and cliffs towered above them.

The storm had wreaked havoc on the
ship. The torn mainsail lay on the deck,
tattered ropes were jumbled in piles and
seawater sloshed in the scuppers. Captain
Gunner, his black frock coat ripped and his

pantaloons gaping at the knee, strode up and down the deck, inspecting the damage. His gaze fell on the boys as they emerged from the hold. "You hopeless little landlubbers!" he bawled. "Come here!"

Al and Jack did as they were told.

"The salt water's got into the biscuits, so there's no food," said Captain Gunner. "You good-for-nothings will have to earn your keep while we fix the ship." He handed the

boys two balls of string with hooks on the ends. "Now catch us some fish."

On top of the cliffs nearby, coconut palms waved in the breeze. "Couldn't we go ashore instead and get some fruit?" Al asked.

Captain Gunner took a step back, his face pale. "That's Death Island. No one goes there. Now get to work or I'm gunner feed you to Greeny Joe."

Al and Jack hung maggoty biscuits from the fish-hooks. But the fish swam by without a glance.

Jack's stomach rumbled loudly. "I'm starving," he said.

Al surveyed the island nearby. With its banana trees and coconuts, he guessed it would bear enough food for all of them. He spied a cave at the foot of the cliffs. Then he looked at *The Booty*'s dinghy. "We could take their dinghy, go through that cave and get some food," he said excitedly.

"I wouldn't if I were you." The boys jumped. They hadn't seen Mahoot come up behind them. "No one who's gone through that cave has ever returned," he told them. "That's why it's called Death Island."

By that evening they still hadn't caught a single fish and hunger pains twisted their guts.

"I don't care what anyone says," Al whispered to Jack. "In the morning I'm taking the dinghy and looking for food."

At first light, Al and Jack crept onto the deck, took a fishing knife and began lowering the dinghy. Mahoot appeared, but when he saw what the boys were doing he ran over to join the them. "If I don't get something to eat soon, I'll be forced to eat my own leg," he said.

Mahoot took the oars and rowed them

to the cave. They landed and hauled the dinghy up from the tideline. Several dark tunnels led into the bowels of the island.

"Which one should we take?" asked Jack.

"First's as good as any," Al replied as he bravely stepped into one of the tunnels. Jack and Mahoot followed, feeling their way in the dark.

"I'll make a mark on the walls," said Al. "It will help us get back."

The tunnel twisted and turned and Al feared they might get lost. He was about to turn back when a dim light ahead caught his eye. Brushing cobwebs aside, the boys rushed forward until Jack stumbled and fell.

Al stopped. "Are you all right?" he asked.

Jack picked something up from the ground and held it out. "I tripped on this," he said. In the weak light, a rotting skull with empty eye sockets leered at them. Horrified, Jack dropped the skull and the

boys sprinted for all they were worth.

They ran into a sheer-walled cavern. The roof had collapsed, creating fingers of gloomy light which illuminated the scene before them.

Skeletons lay strewn over the cavern floor. The stink of rot and decay filled their nostrils.

Al shuddered.

"It's a dead man's cave!" Jack exclaimed in horror.

Mahoot stepped towards a rotting skeleton. "Look, he's been stabbed." His voice echoed eerily.

As Al inspected the carnage, he realised every skeleton was missing a limb or bore a shocking injury. Swords and pistols lay fallen beside their owners. Bony hands clasped sabres.

"Looks like there was a fight between two pirate gangs," said Mahoot.

"I wonder why," said Al.

"Probably fighting over Death Diamond," Mahoot replied. "Legend says it's as big as a duck's egg and it's hidden on this island."

"I can't stand looking at them," Al said, squirming.

Jack's stomach rumbled. "*We'll* drop dead in here too if we don't eat."

"Look, a torch!" cried Mahoot. He picked up a wooden object. "If we find a flint, we can light it and find our way back quickly."

"What's a flint?" asked Al.

Mahoot stared at him. "Where do you come from? Everyone knows what a flint is." He shook his head. "You two are seriously useless."

Since Mahoot didn't answer Al's question, the boys began looking for matches. With a shudder, Al patted a dead man's coat. Nothing.

The next skeleton wore a gold-embroidered
frock coat. A bloodstained knife stuck out
of its chest. Gripped in its rotting hand
was a rolled parchment. Al put his hand in
the pirate's coat pocket. It was empty. He
was about to go to the next body when
something made him pull the parchment
from the pirate's fingers.

He unrolled the paper. It was a map!

Among the blood stains, Death Island and the landing cave were clearly marked, as were several tunnels. The words **diamond** and **Victor** were smudged with age. Al quickly folded the map and put it in his pocket. This was definitely worth keeping.

"Got a flint!" cried Mahoot. He struck what looked like a small rock onto a square stone over the ancient torch. A spark came to life and soon the torch was flaming. Now they had the flaring light the boys turned back to the coast and easily followed the marks Al had left on the twisting tunnels.

Back at the dinghy, their hunger made them try another tunnel. Miraculously, this time they found a stash of bananas and mangoes, and ate until their stomachs were full. Then they loaded the dinghy with fruit and rowed back to the hungry pirates on *The Booty*.

Al was surprised at Captain Gunner's angry glares when they returned. "You boys should be keelhauled!" he growled. "You stole the dinghy. If you hadn't made it back, we'd have lost our lifeboat!"

The crew nodded in agreement.

"You're gunner be punished," he added, as he fell upon the fruit and devoured it with gusto. "Slicer will make sure you don't disobey orders again."

In the galley, Slicer handed the boys scrubbing brushes and bottles of vinegar. "Scrub the floors and make them glow," he said, "and when you've finished, scour the pots and pans." He waved his large knife at them, to show he meant business.

Al, Jack and Mahoot scrubbed the floors till their knuckles ached. "Captain Gunner is unbelievable," Al thought. "We found food for him. Fine reward

we got! I won't show him the treasure
map. He doesn't deserve it."

Later that day, *The Booty* was patched
up. The pirates hauled anchor, and with
billowing sails they departed from Death
Island. But after sailing for a few hours,
another storm hit with a vengeance.

Jack and Al had found their sea legs,
so while Slicer was busy manning the sails,
they went onto the rolling deck to watch
the waves swirl around them and batter the
hull. In the shrieking winds the patched sails
tore apart and flapped thunderously. Al and
Jack wondered if the storm would ever end.
But soon it died down and the ship managed
to limp towards another island.

The Treasure Map

On the coast, a white-walled town glimmered in the evening sunset. The boys' spirits lifted. "We could find a police station and phone home," said Al. But as they approached the shore, their hopes were dashed. Horses pulled carriages, ladies with big skirts walked the cobbled streets and people were lighting oil lamps.

"Are we on a film set, do you think?" said Jack.

"I don't think so," Al replied. "It looks like we're stuck in pirate land. I don't think we're going to find a phone after all."

When they docked, Captain Gunner addressed the crew from the poop deck. "We're gunner be in town for a bit, lads," he said. "We've got no money to go anywhere else." He looked at the boys.

"You two, come with me. I've never seen
such sad faces. You keep that look and you
might make a bit of money begging."
He turned to his bosun. "Mozzy, you and
Slicer go into town and see if you can pick
a few pockets."

"Steal?" cried Jack.

Captain Gunner lifted Jack up by the
collar till his feet came off the ground.
"Steal?" he mimicked. "Of course we're
gunner steal! We're pirates, aren't we?"

Al was outraged. They had just been
punished for borrowing the dinghy but now
they were told they had to beg. He took a
brave step forward. "There's no way we're
going to beg *or* steal," he declared.

Slicer pulled his sword from its scabbard
and pointed it menacingly at Al. "You and
what army will stop us?" he threatened.

Al looked around desperately. He was in a
no-win situation. Jack hung with his feet off

the ground as Captain Gunner shook him like a puppy.

But then Al remembered the map! "There's a better way to get money," he said. "We don't have to rob people." He reached into his pocket. "We could find this treasure." He held the map out to the captain. "I got it from a dead pirate in the caves of Death Island."

Captain Gunner grabbed the map with his spare hand. A huge grin crossed his face. "Changed me mind," he chortled as he let Jack fall to the ground. "No begging or stealing tonight! Instead, I'm gunner get a loan from old Stanley Spong. Then we can have *The Booty* up and running in no time." He smiled at the boys. "You can come with me. Your sad faces might make old Stanley give us a better deal."

A sharp-faced man who smellt like old underpants patted Jack's head. "So these lovely boys found Victor's treasure map." He coughed up some mucus and hawked it into a bowl, then eyed Captain Gunner for a few seconds and said, "I believe you. I'll lend you enough to fix the boat, but I want 300 per cent interest or I'll take your boat and sell the crew for slaves." He glanced at the boys. "And these two'll make good jockeys for the Maharaja's camels."

"You're a bigger pirate than me," Captain Gunner sighed, looking pained. "But as you're the only quick money in town, it's a deal." The two men spat on their palms and shook hands.

When Gunner and the boys left, Stanley waited a few minutes before shutting up shop. He wound his way through some dark alleys until he came to a grimy hotel door. Inside he met a woman with a hat pulled

down over her head so only one side of her face was visible. A drop of moisture hung from her nose which she wiped away with the sleeve of her dress. Stanley leant over and whispered something. She laughed, and her one visible eye glinted greedily. She handed Stanley a handful of money.

When Stanley Spong left, the woman made her way to the docks. She boarded a ship called *The Tormentor*. There, she removed her hat. Her scarred face, which sported an eye patch, told of a terrible injury.

"We sail after treasure," she declared. She turned to a one-legged pirate standing beside her. "Sharkbait, I want one of your dogs to watch *The Booty*. Gunner's found out where the Death Diamond is. Hoist the skull and crossbones and make ready to sail. When Gunner takes off we'll follow – and he'll lead us straight to it."

"Aye, aye," said Sharkbait.

The woman glared furiously at her bosun. "What did you say?"

"Sorry," Sharkbait replied. "I meant, aye, Captain Nell."

"That's better," she said, wiping her nose with the back of her hand.

Dead Men's Cave

All too soon Al, Jack and Mahoot found themselves back in the dead men's cave. Captain Gunner waved the treasure map with glee, oblivious to the skeletons all around him. "The tunnel to the diamond is blocked by this landslide," he said. "We're gunner have to shift the rocks."

After hours of hard labour, the tunnel leading to the diamond appeared. Everyone ran forward and peered into the darkness.

"Now, before we set off, remember there are mantraps everywhere," warned Gunner. "So be careful."

Suddenly, a violent, warlike shriek split the air behind them. Everyone spun around as the cave filled with evil-looking pirates, led by a hideously scarred woman with an eye patch.

"Snotty Nell!" Captain Gunner cried,

as his men drew their weapons. But they were too slow. After a brief scuffle they were completely overpowered.

"Give me the treasure map or I'll slay you all!" Snotty Nell shouted, waving her sword. No one heeded her demand, so she seized Mahoot by the hair, tipped his head back and held her sword against his neck. "Give us the map or I'll slit the boy's throat."

Her actions galvanised Captain Gunner. "Leave him alone," he called out. "It's in my coat pocket. Take it."

Snotty Nell grabbed the treasure map. "The diamond's mine," she crowed triumphantly.

"You'll never find it and live!" yelled Captain Gunner.

Snotty Nell glared at the map. "You're right. There are dangerous mantraps." She thought for a moment, then her eye narrowed. "What I'll do is get you and your crew to help me find the diamond. You can go first and test out the tunnels." She laughed maliciously. "Ain't *I* the generous one!" She turned to her bosun. "Sharkbait, you stay here as you're so slow. Guard some hostages." She pointed to Al and Jack.

Sharkbait wobbled a little on his peg leg as he grabbed the boys and forced them to sit.

Then he dragged Mahoot over and lashed them together with a rope.

"If one of you rascals even thinks of trying to escape," Snotty Nell informed Gunner's crew, "Sharkbait will kill these lovely boys." She poked her sword into the captain's back. "Let's get a move on then," she ordered.

Deathly Dangers

The rope cut into the boys' arms, and
every time one of them moved they hurt
the others. "Try to relax," advised Mahoot.
"It's worse if you wriggle."

Hours went by and the three must have
drifted off to sleep because Al woke when
someone poked him in the chest. Standing
over him was a girl with red hair and a
freckly nose, wearing a long dress with
a knife in the waistband. "Where do *you*

come from?" she asked.

"The twenty-first century," Al replied. He pulled on the ropes to wake Jack and Mahoot.

"Grenda!" Mahoot exclaimed. "I wondered when you'd turn up."

Grenda ignored Mahoot and continued to stare at Al. "You have strange clothes. What are those?" She pointed to Al's shoes.

"Trainers," said Al.

"Trainers?" The girl shrieked with laughter.

Mahoot was laughing now, too.

"Never seen or heard anything so silly," Grenda went on. She turned and looked at Mahoot. "I'm bored. The dead pirates stink. Tell me a story or something."

"I don't want to tell you a story. Where's Sharkbait?" asked Mahoot.

"He's having a feed and a sleep. I'm sick of eating salty beef, so I said I'd guard you."

She poked Al again. "Silly hair," she added. "Looks like it's been chewed by rats. Silly clothes."

"If you're sick of salty beef, we know where there's lots of great fruit," said Al, thinking quickly. "If you want we can take you there."

"No," said Grenda. "I'm supposed to guard you." With those words she walked off to explore the cave. She put a dead pirate's hat on her head and did a little dance. "*Bored, bored, bored*," she sang. After about ten minutes of walking around, she came back. "If I untie you, will you promise not to escape?" she asked.

"Definitely," said Mahoot.

"Pirate's oath?"

"Pirate's oath," said Mahoot. Grenda held her knife in front of Mahoot. He spat on the knife. "May I be eaten by a shark and rot as a ghost if I try to escape," he said.

In turn, Grenda put the knife before Al's
and Jack's lips. They spat and made the same
pledge. Grenda smiled in satisfaction, untied
them and, together, with torches
held high, they made their way out into
the open air.

While Mahoot and Al looked for fruit, Jack taught Grenda how to moonwalk. Her laughter at his antics was infectious.

"She isn't too bad for a pirate's daughter," Mahoot said to Al. "We've met a few times. She's not like her mum, Snotty Nell."

"How did you become a pirate?" Al asked Mahoot.

"I lived with my grandfather on Sabre Island," he replied. "He looks after the elephants there. Anyway, Gunner turned up one day and was going to kill one of the elephants for ivory, but Grandfather begged him to stop. Gunner stopped, but only after he made a deal. He took me as his cabin boy and I've been working for him ever since. He's gone back to the island lots of times and he takes me to visit Grandfather."

"Perhaps you should join up with Snotty's crew," said Al. He turned and looked down the cliffs at *The Tormentor*,

moored alongside *The Booty*. "They sound like they've got better food, and you might be able to go home."

"No way," answered Mahoot. "Snotty Nell is as mean as she is ugly. She's one of the nastiest pirates in all of the Dragon Blood Islands. Gunner's actually a real softy. He acts mean, but he never does anything about it. He's called Gunner, not because he has a gun, but because he's always gunner do stuff and then he never does. Between you and me, he makes sure Grandfather is OK and doesn't go hungry."

"Speaking of hungry," Al said as he spotted some fruit under a large tree, "do you want that mango?"

Mahoot nodded. When the two boys reached the tree, Al noticed an opening near the roots. "What's that?" he said. "It looks like another entrance to the caves."

"You never know, it might lead us to

the diamond," joked Mahoot.

"Is anyone ever really going to find this diamond?" Al said.

"Snotty Nell will if anyone will," replied Mahoot. "Gunner never has any luck. Even Snotty's boat used to belong to Gunner. She stole it from him years ago. He's never forgiven her and they are sworn enemies. She always wins. This time Gunner's done for. He'll lose everything."

"Maybe we could try to find the diamond," Al suggested. "I saw the map. And if we got it, we could save Gunner."

Mahoot smiled. "We could try," he said. He stood up and called out to the others. "Hey, Grenda, Jack! Look! I can see old Sharkbait headed back from *The Tormentor*!"

Grenda stopped what she was doing and ran over to Mahoot. "We'd better hurry," she said breathlessly. "He'll be furious that I've let you out."

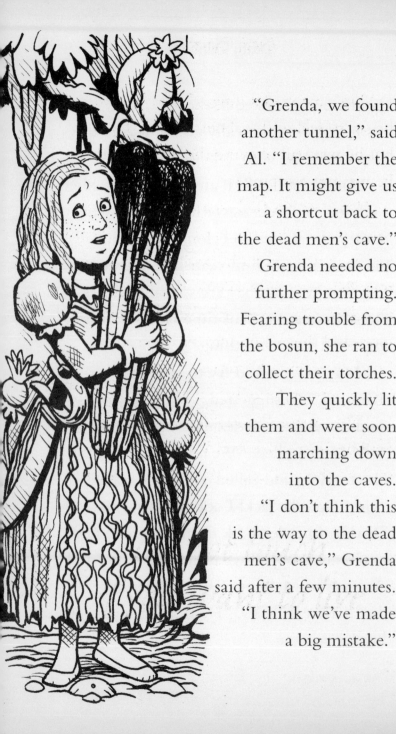

"Grenda, we found another tunnel," said Al. "I remember the map. It might give us a shortcut back to the dead men's cave." Grenda needed no further prompting. Fearing trouble from the bosun, she ran to collect their torches. They quickly lit them and were soon marching down into the caves. "I don't think this is the way to the dead men's cave," Grenda said after a few minutes. "I think we've made a big mistake."

"Just give it a bit longer," said Al. He began to feel guilty about tricking her, but he was still obeying the pirate's oath: he was not escaping.

Their torches flickered on the wet, slimy walls. The tunnel steepened suddenly, and they had to watch every step in case they fell. Soon it levelled out. Ahead, blue twinkling lights radiated a phosphorous glow and they came across a cavern lit by glow-worms. "Amazing," said Jack, awestruck by the sight.

"What's this?" asked Grenda. On the cave wall in front of her was a rusty lever. It was set into the rock and above it was written:

Do not touch
if you want to live

Before Al could work out what the words meant, Grenda pulled the lever. A loud grinding noise made them look up In the eerie light, a giant blade fell from the ceiling. It scythed downwards, then up again in an arched motion, hitting the ceiling above their heads with an intense thud. Grenda, who was in the way, was catapulted into the air. Her bloodcurdling shriek filled the tunnel.

Al shut his eyes, his stomach churning. He didn't want to see Grenda's dead body. But as she kept screaming, Al realised she was alive. He opened his eyes. Grenda hung from the roof, upside down. The blade had swept past her and become caught in her full skirt as it swung upwards.

"Get me down!" Grenda screamed. The boys climbed onto each other's shoulders, removed the knife from her waistband and cut her free. When she had found her feet,

Mahoot took her hand. "You were lucky you weren't killed," he said. "One more millimetre and you'd have been sliced in half!"

"The caves must be full of mantraps," said Al. "We'd better go back and face Sharkbait's anger."

"Yes, let's go," said Jack.

"I shouldn't have touched that lever," Grenda apologised.

"You could have waited till we read the sign," said Al, pointing to the strange words on the cave wall.

"I can't read," she said. "We pirate kids don't go to school."

"Even if you could read," said Jack, defending Grenda, "this is gobbledygook."

"It's code," said Al. "I just need a minute to work it out. It might give us a clue to something." He leant against the wall and was about to say, "I'm pretty good at codes," when the wall gave way.

Like a revolving door, it swung back, rolled around, pushed him into another cave and slammed shut behind him. His friends hammered on the rock, but Al couldn't find the way back to them. Armed only with a fading torch, he soon realised there was nothing for it but to go on alone.

The Diamond's Curse

Al's torch soon burnt out. He staggered through impenetrable darkness, crashing into walls and bumping his head. He choked back the fear that he would die in the tunnels and never see his friends again. Finally, exhausted, he slumped to the floor. He lay there for a minute, steadying the thump of his heart and summoning his courage. "You mustn't stop or give in," he told himself as he stood up.

He was just wondering which way he
should try to walk when he heard a noise.
"It's my mind playing tricks," he told
himself, but then it came again. Voices! He
stumbled towards the sound.

Snotty Nell's torches flickered brightly
against the darkness. "It's a bit confusing
which tunnel we should take," she said as
she turned the map this way and that. She
and her crew stood in a small cavern, which
had several tunnels leading into it.

Death Diamond

Al sneaked towards them and hid behind a rock. *The Booty*'s crew was sitting on the floor, so close to him he could almost touch them. Gunner was nearest to him, guarded by a tall pirate holding a sword to the captain's chest. The tall pirate snarled at his captive, "As soon as we get that diamond, I'm going to be the one who guts you."

Gunner lifted his head defiantly. "Vampire Zu, you're big, but the bigger you are the further you fall."

Vampire Zu kicked Gunner in the leg viciously and smiled a sharp-toothed smile. "You're a dead man," he hissed.

Snotty Nell interrupted their argument. "We're all exhausted, so we'll have a bit of shuteye," she said. "Snuff out your torches and save them for later."

Shortly, everything went black and the pirates' snores told Al they were asleep.

Remembering where Gunner was sitting, Al carefully moved to his side. He tapped him and whispered, "Shhhh, it's Al. I'm going to untie you."

Within minutes, Gunner and his crew were free. Holding hands, they crept away, back down the tunnel Al had just come through. When he was sure they couldn't be heard easily, Gunner whispered, "I'm not letting Snotty have that diamond. We should follow her. We don't have the map and we need it or we could be lost down here forever, diamond or no diamond. We follow her, find the right moment and take the map!"

Gunner and his crew sat quietly in the dark until the lights of the torches told them Snotty was awake. There was a great commotion when Snotty realised her captives had escaped. Gunner's crew waited while the angry pirates argued among themselves. Soon they heard that Snotty and her crew were going to look for the diamond first, then hunt down the escapees later.

Even though Snotty's crew were noisy and argumentative, they were not easy to follow. The twisting tunnels were confusing, and Al shuddered every time he ran into a sticky spiderweb and the hairy creatures scuttled over him. Quite often Gunner's crew stumbled and fell, but not a sound escaped their lips.

Eventually their trek came to an end. Snotty's pirates came out of the tunnel and entered a massive, ghostly cave lit by glow-worms. Gunner and his crew hid in the shadows and let their eyes grow accustomed to the strange light.

In the middle of the cavern, on a large rock, sat piles of gleaming pearls. The pearls were heaped around a huge diamond.

In the light of the glow-worms, the Death Diamond flickered like a star.

Al noticed a gigantic boulder, suspended
at a strange angle just above the diamond.
He studied it further and in the gloom he
made out the wires of a clever pulley system.
The boulder cast a threatening shadow over
the cave.

Snotty's men couldn't believe their greedy
eyes. An echoing cheer came from their
throats. "Fill your pockets!" one of the men
cried, and the pirates stampeded towards
the treasure. In a flash the ground opened
beneath their feet. A great puff of dust and
dirt erupted, and the pirates disappeared.

Smiling, Gunner's pirates left the shadows,
carefully crept to the edge of the huge
mantrap and peered in. Several metres down,
Snotty and her men were wriggling in a
confusion of arms, legs and swords.

Gunner roared down at Snotty Nell.
"The diamond's ours now. Hope your bum
hurts, you old pig!"

Snotty Nell yelled something back but, luckily, all the pirates who had fallen on top of her muffled her reply.

Gunner made a move towards the diamond.

"Gunner, I think there could be more mantraps," Al cried in warning. "I think you should stay here and let me get the diamond. I'm light and I might not set them off."

"Good idea, young Al," Gunner agreed, patting Al on the back warmly. "So far you've been very lucky. You do what you think's best."

Al bravely set off, testing each step before putting his full weight on his feet. He zigzagged slowly across the cavern floor. Eventually the diamond was only centimetres away from his eyes. He looked up at the rock that hung menacingly above the diamond. He stepped back and looked around some more. There, on the stone below the diamond, was an inscription:

Warning: do not move the weight in front of you

It was that code again.

"What's keeping you?" called Gunner.

"It's booby-trapped," replied Al. "There's a clue written here. It'll take me a bit of time to figure it out."

Al thought for a while before he realised what the code said. Then he moved back and returned to the pirate crew. "Find me a rock about the size of a duck's egg," he told them.

Gunner nodded and the men searched the edges of the cave. Eventually a rock was found. Al tested it in his hand. It was about the same size as the diamond. He hoped it was about the same weight. Warily he returned to the diamond. Using all his concentration, he positioned the stone millimetres above and just beside the diamond. Then, careful not to move even one pearl with his sleeve, he snatched the diamond and immediately put the rock in its place. For a second the giant boulder above him wobbled, but then it settled. With the diamond gleaming in his hand, he held it high.

Stealing Ships

Captain Gunner jumped around with joy.
He patted the diamond in his pocket and
his huge grin made his eyes twinkle. "Al,"
he said, laughing, "Al, you are just the best."
He grabbed Al's hand and shook it hard.
"I'm nearly the happiest man in the world
and I'm soon to be even happier." He
beckoned Al to follow him as he made his
way to the mantrap. Snotty Nell and
her crew stood forlornly at the bottom.

Captain Gunner called out to the pirates below. "You can rot down there! I'm gunner leave you to die!"

"You festering pimple!" cried Snotty Nell. "I'll make you pay."

"Don't know how," replied Captain Gunner. "You rapscallions won't be getting out of that hole, especially you, Vampire Zu." With those words he stepped back from the trap and stamped his feet, like he was walking away. He suppressed a huge smile.

"You're not leaving us!" cried Snotty Nell. "You wouldn't leave us to die?"

"Do you give in?" Gunner called back. "Will you promise not to escape and also say we are the best pirates and you are just a scabby crew of lickspittles?"

"*Never!*" screamed Snotty Nell.

"Die then," said Gunner. He put his finger to his lips for silence. No one moved.

The seconds ticked by as Snotty Nell thought about the situation.

"All right. We promise!" she yelled, still furious.

"And?" asked Gunner.

"We're lickspittles," cried Snotty Nell angrily. "Now let us out."

"What are you?" Gunner asked.

"Scabby lickspittles," Snotty Nell replied reluctantly. "Now can we come out...please?"

"I'm a fool to myself," Gunner answered. "Throw up all your weapons and we'll haul you out."

The roles had reversed. Snotty Nell and her crew were the prisoners now. *The Booty*'s crew marched behind them, back to the dead men's cave, with their swords drawn.

Hours later, the victorious crew of *The Booty* emerged from the tunnels to find Jack and Mahoot tied together and Grenda sitting in a corner as punishment for letting the boys escape. Sharkbait was stalking up and down, keeping guard. There was a cry of relief from the boys at the sight of Al, safe and sound. As Sharkbait was overpowered and Grenda rushed into her mother's arms, Al untied his friends.

Grenda glared fiercely at Al. "I'm never going to forgive you," she snapped.

It wasn't long before Captain Gunner made *The Tormentor* his home again. He set the sails and the sleek frigate flew across the ocean, leaving Death Island behind them. He left Snotty Nell and her crew on the island. *The Booty* was left at anchor, but not before Gunner cut the sails and ropes with his sword. He took out a spyglass and watched his old boat until it disappeared over the horizon. "We're not gunner see them again," he said.

Little known to Gunner, though, Snotty Nell was busy at work. Sharkbait had not wasted his time while the other pirates were looking for the diamond. He had kept himself busy in the dead men's cave, collecting all the skeletons' sabres, swords, knives and pistols, and hiding them, just in case they were needed one day. When he told Snotty Nell of his work, her face broke out in a rare smile.

Once Captain Gunner had sailed away, Snotty's crew picked up the weapons and stripped the fine coats from the skeletons of the dead pirates. With needles and thread they set to work and patched *The Booty*'s sails. Soon a colourful rig was flapping in the breeze. As *The Booty* set sail, Snotty Nell placed a hand on her daughter's shoulder. "We'll sneak up on Gunner tonight," she said. "And I'll make him sorry."

"But aren't you glad he didn't leave you down in the pit?" Grenda asked.

Her mother glared at her. "I worry about you, my girl," she replied. "You're a poor excuse for a pirate. I thought you'd want revenge on those scamps who tricked us all."

Grenda smiled at her mother. "They were annoying," she agreed, but secretly she thought about the fun she'd had with the boys. Sometimes it was very boring being the only kid on a pirate ship. "I'm just glad they didn't leave you to die," she said aloud.

"True," her mother said. "For that small mercy, I won't kill them when I catch up with them. I'll just get what should be mine."

That night, in town, Gunner sold the diamond for a trunk of gold doubloons. He repaid his loan to Stanley Spong and gave every crew member an equal share of the treasure. "It's a party on board *The Tormentor* tonight," he told them joyously.

"I'll make salmagundi, the most delicious pirate stew," said Slicer. "You can't have a party without salmagundi. And I'll use my gold to buy all the best ingredients. What will you boys do with your money?"

"Not sure," replied Al, as he stared at his mountain of gold coins on the galley table. Snakeboot the cat mewed and jumped up.

"We could at least get a cat box for old Snakeboot," said Jack, tickling the cat under the chin. "He needs a better place to sleep than on the floor. It gets so wet during the storms."

The boys pocketed some of their gold coins and went shopping. Mahoot bought himself some shoes and a new pair of trousers. Jack and Al found a carved wooden box for Snakeboot and carried it back to the boat.

While they were helping get ready for the party, Al looked at their pile of gold coins. "Where will we keep them all?" he asked. "If I was at home I'd put them in the bank, but there's no bank here..."

"Bank?" asked Mahoot.

"It's a place where you can put money and people look after it for you so it can't be stolen," answered Jack. "And if you want to get money out you just put a card in a hole in the wall and the money pops out."

Mahoot shook his head in disbelief. "You boys come from some strange place," he said. "Around here, we'd just hide it."

"In Snakeboot's cat box," Al suddenly suggested. "He'll guard it."

Snakeboot pressed his head against Al in agreement, so the boys put their gold coins in the bottom of the cat box and put a blanket over the top. The cat leapt inside and purred.

Slicer made pirate stew. Into a giant pot he threw mangoes, anchovies, half a pig chopped into pieces, a tub of pickled herrings, four cabbages, onions, olives, grapes and two giant fish, bones and all, then added garlic, salt, pepper and mustard to improve the taste.

"No way am I eating *that*," said Al, as his nose twisted at the atrocious smell of salmagundi.

"I'd vomit," agreed Jack. So the boys made themselves an omelette and helped themselves to bread.

As the sky grew dark, the ship's navigator got out his fiddle, Mozzy found a drum and Slicer had a flute. A small band was soon playing sea shanties and the pirates sang

and danced, while gorging themselves on
the salmagundi.

"You'd have to be tough to eat that," said
Al in admiration.

Eventually the pirates wore themselves
out and everyone fell asleep happy and
contented.

Al was dreaming he was back at home
in his nice sitting room watching TV
when he was suddenly pulled to his feet.
Vampire Zu's angry eyes bore into him.
Al tried to shout a warning but the man's
giant hand forced his mouth shut and fierce
fingers dug into his neck. Al struggled
bravely but he was gagged, bound and
pushed to the floor. He watched in dismay
as Jack and Mahoot and the rest of the
crew were also captured.

Snotty Nell arrived and stole any
gold coins she could find. She went to

Snakeboot's cat box and tried to haul the cat out. Snakeboot bristled, hissed and lashed out with his front paw, cutting deeply into Snotty Nell's hand. "Foul fiend!" she shrieked, sucking the blood. She beckoned Sharkbait over. "You pull it out," she ordered.

Sharkbait made a move towards the cat, but Snakeboot sprang at the pirate's head and attacked, kicking hard with his back feet and slicing at his face.

Sharkbait screamed and jumped away, and the cat returned to his box, his purple eyes glaring savagely.

"I'm not touching it," Sharkbait said. "Leave the creepy thing where it is."

"*You* kill it," Snotty ordered Vampire Zu.

Vampire Zu looked closely at the cat and paled. "Look at its eyes," he said, and a shiver went down his spine. "I'd be cursed if I touched it."

"Pack of no-hopers," said Snotty Nell. "Pick it up, box and all, and put it on board *The Booty*. I don't want the horrid thing left on *my* boat."

So Snakeboot and Gunner's trussed-up crew were carried onto *The Booty* and left on deck.

Snotty Nell waved a cheery goodbye as she sailed off in *The Tormentor* with all the gold.

Saved

The pirates lay on the deck of *The Booty*,
bound and gagged. Al wriggled like a snake
over to Jack and put his face to Jack's hands.
Jack understood Al's plan and pulled at his
gag with his fingers until it loosened. With
his teeth free, Al chewed and pulled at the
ropes holding Jack's hands. His jaw ached
as he worked, but the big knots began to
move. Soon Jack was free, along with the
rest of the crew.

"Hell's bells and buckets of blood," swore Captain Gunner sadly as he looked around his boat. "We're ruined. She's even taken our weapons, the mean old trout."

Slicer patted Gunner's shoulder. "We'll get her yet," he said. "We'll feed her to Greeny Joe, you can bet."

Gunner brightened. "That shark did a good job on her once," he agreed. "But even if Greeny ate her tonight, we're sunk. No money, no food and no weapons." As he spoke, Snakeboot came on deck and wrapped himself around Captain Gunner's leg. Gunner absent-mindedly reached down and patted the cat.

"We're not ruined," Al told him. "Snakeboot's got a fortune."

When Gunner saw the boys' gold, his eyes popped out. "I can't take that," he told them. "That's yours by pirate law, and pirate crews don't take things from each other."

"We can't be a
crew if you don't
fix the ship and
buy new weapons,
and then you could
take me to see
my grandfather,"
Mahoot suggested.

"It's a deal," said
Captain Gunner
gratefully. "I told
everyone you'd
be lucky and you
sure have been."
He tickled
Snakeboot behind
the ear. "And
you're the best
mascot a pirate
ship has ever had!"

Hours later, Jack and Al went into town to do a bit of exploring, but Snakeboot followed them. When they were a long way from the boat, Jack saw him. "Hey, Snakeboot," said Jack. "What are you doing here?"

"We'd better pick him up and take him back," said Al. "He might get lost." Al bent to pick up Snakeboot, but the cat dodged and ran down a winding alley. The boys ran after him.

Snakeboot stopped outside a crumbling warehouse. Broken windows, grime and spiderwebs told the boys the building was abandoned. The cat leapt up at the door. "He wants to go in there," Jack said.

Al tried the door but it was locked. The cat mewed and clawed at the door again, so the boys looked around for another way in. Above the door was a sign:

Alleric Traders

"Same name as you, Al," Jack said. "Alleric. It's a strange name, isn't it?"

Al nodded. "It was my grandfather's name. He was Alleric and I was named after him. I don't really like it, though."

"Well, Snakeboot wants to go in," said Jack. "How can we help him?"

Snakeboot leapt against the door, this time quite desperately.

"We could ask someone if they've got a key," suggested Al. As he said the word 'key', he remembered the key to his grandfather's trunk, which was still in his pocket.

He pulled it out. It looked like it would fit. He put the key in the keyhole and turned it. The door opened.

The boys stepped inside and suddenly goosebumps went up and down Al's spine. He shut his eyes.

Al was standing in the attic at home with
Jack beside him. Their drinks were on
the floor where they had left them. Al
picked up his cola. It was still cold. His
father's voice came from downstairs.
"Alleric Breas, this is the last time I'm
going to ask you to come down and
help with the dishes!"

Al stared at Jack. Jack stared at Al.

"Did we just go to pirate land?" Al asked.

"Maybe it was all in our imagination,"
said Jack.

"AL BREAS!" Al's dad shouted. "Come
downstairs *now.*"

"Definitely our imagination," said Al. "I
really should help Dad with the dishes."

"I should go home," said Jack, still
in shock.

Just then, Al's sister, Hally, stuck her head
into the attic. "Dad's getting mad," she
warned her brother. Then her eyes went

wide. "Where did you get that cat?"

The boys turned. Their eyes bugged out in total disbelief. Snakeboot was standing beside the trunk!

"Oh, the poor thing has lost its paw," said Hally. "And it looks so fluffy and furry." She patted the cat. "Is it a stray?"

Both boys nodded, dumbfounded, unable to find their voices.

"I'll take it down to show Dad. He'll let me keep it!" said Hally.

The cat purred loudly, rolled over and showed its tummy. "You can be my little snickerpoo-face kitty," Hally cooed as she rubbed the cat's underbelly. "Oooh, feel its fur. It's so soft! And you are so white, just like a little ghost. I'll call you Furghost, won't I, shnookums?" She gave the cat a kiss on the nose. "No, that's not a good name. You need a nice name. How about Furgus?"

"She's calling Snakeboot 'Furgus'!" whispered Jack.

Al shook his head. "I don't want to talk about it just now," he replied. "I think I should go and do the dishes."

So Jack and Al went back to their everyday lives. But they couldn't help wondering when they might have their next pirate adventure...

Clues to the Puzzles

The messages on pages 55 and 67 are in
mirror writing. Hold each page in front of
a mirror to work out what the messages say.
If you're still in doubt, log on to
www.dragonbloodpirates.co.uk
for the answers.

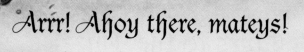

Arrr! Ahoy there, mateys!

hoist the sails and drop the anchor: ye have some treasure to find!

One swashbucklin' reader will win a haul of booty, including an Xbox console and games and an iTunes voucher, and twelve runners up will win a Dragon Blood Pirates booty bag.

For a chance to win, ye must dare to unearth the treasure using the Dragon Blood Islands map from *Death Diamond* (also available to download at www.dragonbloodpirates.co.uk), and the six big pirate stickers that are inserted in every book.

Each of the six Dragon Blood Pirates books contains a clue revealing an island protected by a dastardly pirate, and a sticker of the pirate to place on your map. When ye have solved the six clues, and have placed the six stickers, there will remain only one island, where the pirate booty be.

To win, enter online at
www.dragonbloodpirates.co.uk

Or send your name, address and the name of the island where the treasure lies to:

**Dragon Blood Pirates Treasure Hunt
338 Euston Road, London NW1 3BH**

Best o' luck, me hearties!

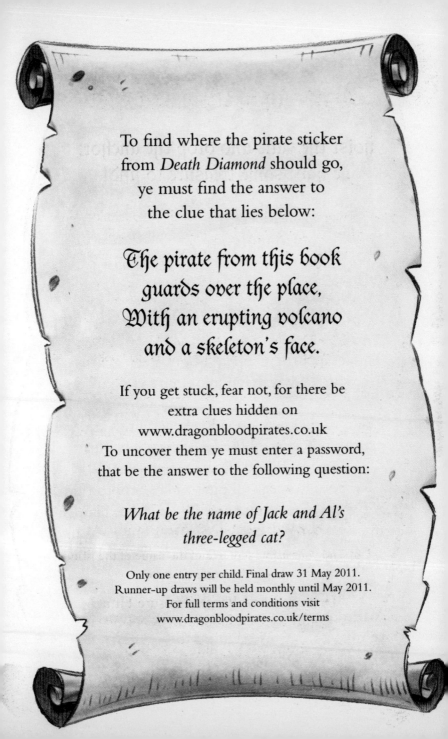

To find where the pirate sticker
from *Death Diamond* should go,
ye must find the answer to
the clue that lies below:

**The pirate from this book
guards over the place,
With an erupting volcano
and a skeleton's face.**

If you get stuck, fear not, for there be
extra clues hidden on
www.dragonbloodpirates.co.uk
To uncover them ye must enter a password,
that be the answer to the following question:

*What be the name of Jack and Al's
three-legged cat?*

www.dragonbloodpirates.co.uk

Ahoy there shipmates!

To reel in amazin' pirate booty, steer smartly
towards www.dragonbloodpirates.co.uk

Ye'll find games, downloads, activities and
sneak previews of the latest swashbucklin'
Dragon Blood Pirates adventures.
Learn how to speak all pirate-like, how to find
out what type of pirate ye be, an' what pirate
games ye can play with yer mates! This treasure
trove is a sure feast fer yer deadlights!

Only the bravest an' heartiest amon' ye
can become a true scurvy dog, so don't
ye miss a thing and sign up to yer newsletter
at www.dragonbloodpirates.co.uk!

Don't ye miss book two in the

Dragon Blood Pirates

series!

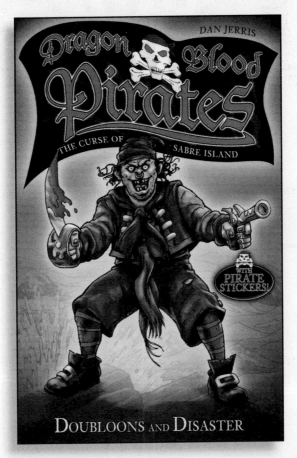

Turn the page and shiver yer timbers
with a slice of the next high-seas adventure...

Buried Treasure

"We must be back in the Dragon Blood
Islands!" cried Alleric Breas. He was
crouched behind some sand dunes
watching a red-coated pirate. Waving
a nine-tailed whip, the pirate stood on a
wreck, which gleamed with fresh paint.
Its sails, although torn, still flapped in the
breeze. Several other pirates were pulling the
wreck apart, flinging timbers into the water.
The red pirate's voice carried in the wind.

"You sspineless layaboutss. Work fasster. Find that treasure, or it'll be the cat-o'-nine-tailss across your backss."

"At least we're on land this time," said Jack Seabrook, Al's friend. "And there's no shark."

Al shuddered at the memory of their last adventure. He and Jack had been playing in his attic at number five Drake Drive, when they had come across his grandfather's old sea trunk. They'd opened the lid and, within seconds, found themselves in the middle of the ocean. They'd been rescued by some pirates from a huge shark and survived a kidnapping before they were suddenly returned home. But now they were back again!

Al looked at the scene in front of him. "That wrecked ship looks brand new," he observed, "so something bad must have happened to the crew. We'd better be careful."

"I'm beginning to wish we'd stayed in your bedroom," said Jack. "We shouldn't have gone into the attic and opened that trunk again."

"But Snakeboot was clawing at it," said Al. He reached out and tickled the ears of the three-legged white cat beside him. "I had to see what he wanted. So when he jumped into the trunk, I looked in to see where he went. I didn't plan to come back here."

"I know," said Jack, "and I couldn't just stand there after you had disappeared. I had to follow you."

"I don't like the look of those pirates," said Al.

"Neither do I," agreed Jack. "Can we go straight back home?"

"Let's try." Al patted the cat. "Come on, Snakeboot, show us how to get back to the twenty-first century. There's a good cat."

Snakeboot seemed to understand. Purring, he headed away from the beach and the pirates. He followed a jungle path, where monkeys chattered from the trees and a large yellow snake slithered between Al's legs, making him jump. "Argh! We better keep our eyes peeled," he warned, as Snakeboot leapt ahead.

Eventually, the cat stopped in a clearing, just behind another beach. "We must be on an island," said Al, "but I don't think it's one of the islands we visited last time, with Captain Gunner and his crew."

Snakeboot sniffed at some freshly turned earth in the clearing. He began to dig a hole in the soft ground. When he was satisfied, he squatted. "Great," said Jack. "We came all this way just so the cat could go to the loo."

When Snakeboot finished, he scratched the soil again, but this time unearthed a gold coin. Al picked it up. "It's a doubloon!" he said. "I wonder if this is part of the treasure those pirates on the beach are looking for?"

"I wonder what happened to the crew of that ship?" said Jack. "Do you think the pirates killed them?"

"I didn't see a lifeboat on the wreck," said Al. "So if the people on the ship were being chased by pirates, perhaps they panicked, ran aground, abandoned ship and rowed ashore in the lifeboat. They might have buried the treasure and then escaped, hoping to come back some day."

"Still, finding a gold coin from some buried treasure doesn't help us get home," said Jack.

"Perhaps it can," said Al. "We can't stay here, so which way should we go? Heads, left; tails, right." He tossed the coin into the air.

"Tails," said Jack. The coin spun and dropped.

"Tails it is," said Al. "So we go right." He tossed the coin to Jack, who put it in his pocket.

Jack hoped that somehow the doubloon would bring them luck – and get them safely back home soon...

Captured by Pirates

Hours later, after walking to the right, the boys were back at the beach where they'd started – feeling tired, thirsty and hungry. The wrecked ship lay empty, the pirates nowhere to be seen. Still, the boys ducked down, crept to the edge of the beach and scanned it for any signs of danger.

Suddenly, Snakeboot's fur bristled and the cat hissed a warning. Jack and Al turned their heads. Standing behind them was a boy, about the same age as them, but a bit taller and heavier. "What are you two doing here?" he asked. His mocking grin flashed brightly.

The boys stood up to reply, but the newcomer put his hand to his mouth and called, "Hey, Blacktooth! I've just found two of the crew from the ship we've been chasing!"

In seconds, a grim band of pirates surrounded the boys. The red pirate with the whip smiled cruelly, exposing one black tooth that clung to his lower jaw. He came over and picked Al up by his collar. "By the lookss of your odd clothess, I'd guesss you've come off that foreign ssloop there," he said, pointing to the wreck.

"No, we're not from that ship," said Al, shaking his head frantically. But as soon as he spoke, Al knew he'd made a mistake.

The red pirate's face darkened in anger. "I hate liarss," he spat. He grabbed Al's arm and twisted it painfully behind his back.

"We know you had treasure on board. And we want to know where it is."

"Yeah, where is it?" the pirate boy said, pushing Jack roughly. Jack fell back onto the sand with a grunt and the gold doubloon in his pocket spilled out.

"Captain Blacktooth," the boy said as he picked up the coin, "I think we have a couple of sneaky spies here."

Blacktooth moved closer to Al and, with his stinking breath fanning Al's face, he shouted, "Where'ss the resst of your crew and where'ss the treasure?"

"It's on the other side of the island," said Jack, before Al had time to answer.

Jack and Al led the pirates to the clearing where they'd found the coin. The pirates began digging and, to their delight, soon found a sea trunk. Grinning, Blacktooth forced open the lock with the knife hanging from a sash on his chest. Inside, golden doubloons and jewellery glinted in the sunshine. "Besst day'ss work in a long time," Blacktooth said. "Pigface, you carry the chesst to the ship!"

A massive, sour-looking pirate with a ring through his nose heaved the trunk to

his shoulders. Then Blacktooth studied Al and Jack for a few minutes and added, "You two liarss could be usseful. I'm sure your family will pay a ranssom for you. While we wait for them to turn up, you can work for me on *The Revenge*."

"Or we could sell them to Stanley pong," said the boy. "He'd pay a pretty penny for them."

Blacktooth smiled evilly. "Good idea, Flash," he agreed. "We'd get a reward quicker that way."